VIENNA

VIENNA

YEARS AGO

TOM JOYCE

Illustrations by
Sonny Heston

authorHOUSE®

AuthorHouse™
1663 Liberty Drive
Bloomington, IN 47403
www.authorhouse.com
Phone: 1-800-839-8640

Published by AuthorHouse 11/19/2014

ISBN: 978-1-4969-5442-8 (sc)
ISBN: 978-1-4969-5443-5 (hc)
ISBN: 978-1-4969-5441-1 (e)

Library of Congress Control Number: 2014920876

CONTENTS

BOOK ONE

A Man and a Woman in a Train Station

Vienna West Train Station—Monday, August 25, 1947

An officious young Viennese man, a minor clerk in the burn center at the Vienna General Hospital, stood with awkward stiffness. When he spoke, it was in English, but he included the conventional Viennese words used to address a woman doctor. "I wish you a good three-day visit to Paris, *Frau Doktor Marbach.*"

Pamela Marbach was a doctor in the British Burn Center in the Vienna General Hospital, but she was also a major in the British Army, and since she was wearing her major's uniform, the young clerk might have addressed her as *Frau Major Marbach.* Sitting beside Pamela Marbach on a wooden bench in the West Train Station of Vienna was her husband, Vienna Police Inspector Karl Marbach.

Dr. Pamela Marbach came to Vienna with the Royal British Medical Corps in mid-1945, shortly after the end of the war in Europe. She was in Vienna for only a few days when she met and quickly fell in love with the police inspector. They were married less than one month after they met.

Now, two years later, Dr. Marbach was still with the Royal British Medical Corps in Vienna. Many people assumed she was British, but she wasn't. She was an American who joined the Royal British Medical Corps in early 1942 after her first husband, the good man to whom she had been married for almost twenty years, was killed while serving on Bataan. His death left her consumed by a need to get into the war and serve the best way she could— which meant serving as a doctor. But back in 1942, the US military wasn't giving commissions to women doctors. So like a few other American women doctors, she joined up with the British and got a commission with the Royal British Medical Corps. She ended up practicing her profession on the battlefields of North Africa, Italy, France, and finally Germany. In recognition of what she did on battlefields, she was awarded a DSO, the combat medal valued more highly than any British combat medal except the Victoria Cross.

Pamela Marbach knew she would always grieve for the husband killed in the Pacific. She could dissolve into tears when she spent even a few moments thinking about that good man. She wondered if she was unique—after all this time, painfully aware of herself as a widow while totally and completely in love with the man who, for the past two years, had been her husband, her lover ... her everything.

At this moment in the West Train Station, the young clerk continued to stand with awkward stiffness.

"Thank you," Pamela Marbach said. She didn't address the clerk by name. She was embarrassed that she couldn't recall the name. It was bad manners to not know his name. It was especially bad manners to not know his name in Vienna.

The officious young clerk made a slight bowing motion and, with an awkward walking style, went on his way.

"His name is Julius Moreau," Police Inspector Karl Marbach said in the English he usually spoke when alone with his wife. "If you couldn't remember his name, you could always have addressed him as 'Herr Clerk.'" Karl Marbach followed those words with a chuckling sound.

Pamela Marbach was used to being teased by her husband. "Oh, pooh," she said.

"Oh, Pammy," Karl Marbach said in reply.

Pammy liked hearing the various Viennese inflections Karl used whenever he pronounced her name. There was one set of inflections when he called her "Pammy," and a slightly different set of inflections when he called her "Dr. Pammy."

Pammy loved Karl. Usually she called him "Karl," but sometimes, when she felt it served her purpose, she called him "Herr Police Inspector." It served her purposes to do that when he addressed her as "Frau Doktor Marbach."

"Tell me, Pammy," Karl said, "that young clerk mentioned Captain Burke. You have never

7

introduced me to Captain Burke. I hear he is most handsome. Who is this handsome Captain Burke who is asking you to join him in Paris?"

Pammy put mock petulance into her voice. "Oh, don't be cute! Captain Burke is an idiot, and he's at least a dozen years younger than me."

Pammy was in her midforties. She fretted about the dark circles under her eyes, and she had always felt her cheeks were too round. Most certainly she had lost the freshness of youth, but odd as it seemed to her, in recent years—during the war and now afterward—she was finding that men seemed much more likely to convey appreciation for her as a woman than had been the case when she was younger. She liked the feeling of being appreciated by men—didn't take advantage, but liked it.

Pammy cast an appreciative glance at Karl. She knew he was faithful to her. She knew for certain he was faithful to her because at the beginning of their love life, he had told her he would always be faithful, and although he sometimes spoofed her, he never lied to her. No lies, no falsehoods, not even any fibs. He never lied about anything. Not to her, not to anybody as far as she could tell. There were many things he avoided talking to her about. She didn't like his way of avoiding talking with her about certain things, but she found it remarkable that he never lied to her. On small things, day-to-day trivia, she might lie to him, but he never lied to her. Sometimes she would tell a lie to keep him from thinking she needed something, or so he wouldn't plan for them to go somewhere she didn't want to go. Occasionally, she would do some fibbing to avoid talking about something she didn't want to talk about. But not the police inspector—not him. He didn't lie and didn't even fib. If there wasn't a spoof going on, he told the absolute truth or kept silent. She might tell him he looked good when he returned from one of his police cases exhausted, unshaved, messy, but he never said she looked good when she showed up after a day or two of intense hospital work, feeling worn out and knowing she looked awful.

Pammy stared at Karl. He was reading the English language magazine he had purchased for her to read on the train trip to Paris. She wanted him to put the magazine away and pay attention to her. She wanted this time between them, before her departure to Paris, to be intimate. Recently, she had become aware of a barrier growing up between them. They'd been having a lot of arguments recently. All of the arguments were connected with her son's upcoming wedding in the United States.

Pammy regarded it as unfair of Karl to be obtuse about how important it was for her to attend the wedding. Of course there would be a lot of expense, and even with two incomes, finances were a problem for them in 1947 Vienna. And of course Karl would have to stay behind in Austria while she was gone for a week. But why was he so disinclined to talk with her about her need to go to the wedding?

Pammy held a newspaper in her trembling hands. Her hands were trembling because she was feeling anger. She grasped the newspaper fiercely, held it up close to her face. The news in the newspaper—as always these days—was bad. A darkening cloud was spreading a shadow over Europe. In recent weeks, there had been Communists killing priests in Yugoslavia, and a death sentence for the anti-Communist leader Nikola Petkov in Bulgaria. In Hungary, things were bad. Red threats had forced

Dezso Sulyok, leader of the Liberty Party, to flee. And closer to home, back last spring there had been food riots in Vienna that for a while had threatened to result in a Communist overthrow of the government.

Europe was facing the prospect of a famine. That famine, if it came, might change everything forever. Combine Communism with a famine, and the forecast was forbiddingly dark.

Pammy put aside the newspaper. Yes, terrible things were happening, but she couldn't do anything about the terrible things. She couldn't even do much about her own personal problems. She stole a glance at Karl. At the very least, there was one piece of business they might talk about before she left on this trip.

She kept her voice firm so there would be no mistaking how important this was to her. Leo Lechner was one of her patients. "Karl, I had another long talk with Leo Lechner. I know you don't like him, but this is important to me. I want you to see Leo. It would mean a lot to me if you would go and see him."

The reply was delivered firmly and directly. "I knew Leo Lechner when he and I were police officers together before the war. I had no use for him then, and I have no use for him now."

"Was Leo Lechner a monster?" Pammy bristled as she continued. "Did he do something awful to you?"

"To me, Leo never did anything."

"Then …?"

"Leo was like all the other young Nazis. The only difference was that he was more energetic than most."

Pammy was silent for a moment. How could she explain? Words seemed futile. She was a Jew—proud of being a Jew. And she hated Nazism with a fury she was sure Karl couldn't possibly imagine, but Leo—the mutilated former Nazi—had managed to touch her with the sincerity of his repentance.

"People change," Pammy said, keeping her voice level and firm. "Leo has been through a lot. I like him. I think maybe you would too, if you got to know him again."

"I hear Leo was badly burned."

Pammy spoke her reply abrasively. "I work in the burn center."

"If it's important to you, I will see any of your patients, even a miserable rat like Leo Lechner."

"Leo is no rat. If he was when you knew him, he has changed. It can happen. People can change."

"Why is it that you and I never bicker? Do you ever wonder about that?"

Pammy delivered a gasping sound. "What do you mean we never bicker? That's what we're doing right now."

"Oh ..."

"And this bickering could turn into a fight. Have you forgotten all those dishes I broke yesterday? You're lucky I didn't break some of them over your head!"

"I have never been able to understand your incredible proclivity for breaking glassware."

Pammy felt her temper flare, but in the next moment, the soft, gentle voice of Karl wiped her anger away.

"Pammy … Pammy. You were right picking fights with me recently, and you were right about deciding to go to America to be at your son's wedding. That is two months from now. Things are fixed. I will be going with you."

For a moment, Pammy had trouble taking a breath. Karl was saying he would be going with her to her son's wedding. It was difficult for her to keep her voice under control. "You'll go with me? But that would cost a fortune. And you're an Austrian citizen. With no passport. How ..."

Aware that they were in the very public West Train Station, Pammy resisted the impulse to shout. Instead of shouting, she bolted into an upright sitting position and spoke in a clear, direct manner. "If you didn't mind me going, if you ... if you were working on a way to come with me, why did we have to have all those fights?" A peculiar rage threatened to ignite within her, but when she looked at Karl's face, all of the fury drained out of her.

Pammy stared at Karl while he said, "You needed to get angry about something. You were getting too wound up with your work. I have my sources at the hospital. They tell me you keep things bottled up. And with me, even when you shout a bit, you always seem to back away rather than keep coming on. Your son is the only thing I've ever seen you willing to really fight with me about. A woman with all of your determination needs to know she can get angry when she's in the right, or even if she just thinks she's in the right. Besides, I needed time to see what could be worked out."

Pammy clutched Karl's arm, but she immediately resolved to not let him get away with feeling smug and superior. "I think I'll have to check this out with your nephew, the priest. I'm not sure you're allowed to go to a Jewish religious service, a Jewish wedding."

Karl delivered a contrived exclamation of surprise. "You never said your son is going to be married at a Jewish ceremony. Imagine that! I suppose they'll be breaking glass. Is it from going to Jewish ceremonies that you got your disregard for glassware?"

"You're a *beast*!" After that exclamation, Pammy took a moment before saying, "I may let you accompany me to the States, but I'm not sure I'll let you come to my son's wedding." She laughed in the deliberately expressive way she knew Karl liked to hear her laugh, and she snuggled her head tight against his chest. She didn't care if they were in a public place. At this moment, she liked snuggling up close.

"You always laugh in E-flat," Karl said to Pammy. Two years ago, on the first day they met, he had told her that laughter in E-flat was his favorite female sound.

While Pammy laughed more of her carefully pitched E-flat laughter, Karl said, "I understand there are marvelous mountains in America. Maybe I'll climb one of your American mountains."

Pammy stopped laughing. "You are much too large a man to be a mountaineer. I have climbed with you. I have seen how you climb, and I have seen how the good mountaineers climb. The best of them are compact, not big characters like you."

"Compact?"

"Yes, like the great French climber, Henri Sampeyre."

Karl examined that remark for a moment. When he spoke, he identified the Frenchman by the first name. "Henri will be in Vienna next week. I have told him he is invited to dinner."

"*Yes!* Oh, yes."

"That Frenchman certainly has a way of impressing women."

"He is a lovely, lovely man." Pammy made a cooing sound and then said, "Oh … be still, my heart."

"Compared to Henri, am I too large or too ugly?"

"Mostly too large."

"Mostly?"

Pammy didn't want to talk any more about Henri Sampeyre. Not after learning Karl would be going with her to her son's wedding. She felt like she was filled with words, words that demanded an outlet. But she couldn't speak. She found herself thinking about the time, three months ago, when her twenty-two-year-old son, Sammy, and his bride-to-be, the young woman named Jennifer, had come to Vienna. Sammy, who would always be bound to his father who had died on Bataan at the beginning of the war, was initially wary of Vienna Police Inspector Karl Marbach. But early on the day Sammy and Jennifer showed up in Vienna, before wariness had a chance to get entrenched, Karl took Sammy out "to see the town." Just the two of them together. Pammy and the bride-to-be were not included. Late in the afternoon when Karl and Sammy came back, they were laughing and joking together. One thing was obvious: they'd had a lot to drink.

Some glassware was broken because of that inebriated return. Pammy tossed dish after dish from the kitchen cabinet onto the floor, but to no effect. Sammy smiled sheepishly, kissed his bride-to-be, and trundled off to his solitary bed in his private bedroom.

After that, Karl attempted to clean up the broken glass, but he cut his hand, and the bride-to-be became his attentive nurse. The blood from the wound could barely be seen on the handkerchief feverishly administered by the moon-faced, young woman named Jennifer. The final outrage for Pammy came when her rugged police inspector husband croaked that he was beginning to feel a little faint. There had been nothing for her to do but retire for the night. So she stalked off to their room. A few minutes later, when Karl was still downstairs, she went to the

bedroom door and hollered for him until he came
to bed.

That was three months ago. Now, sitting in the
Vienna West Train Station, Pammy thought about
the days that followed that first encounter with
Jennifer. The plain and simple fact of the matter
was that she didn't have a high opinion of the young
woman. She told Karl that the young bride-to-be
was too girlish to be getting married to Sammy.

But things quickly changed. And it was all Karl's
doing. He arranged a mountain climbing adventure.
Before the climb, he spent two days teaching Sammy
and Jennifer how to do mountain climbing.

Then came the climb. A climb up the Dolomite
Alps. The four of them used a cable car to get to a
starting place where they began a five-hour climb

high upward, fighting snow and ice. It was a grand climb! Even though the weather turned bad, they kept going until they were only a dozen meters down from the top.

It was then that Karl, leading the climb, signaled for Jennifer to come forward. He whispered something to her and shoved her upward.

On her own, Jennifer made her way the rest of the way to the top. When she got to the top, she jumped with happiness and hollered for the stragglers to "catch up."

All of the climbing, especially the final part of the climb, had left Pammy filled with joy. It had been especially grand for her to hear the wonderful young woman call for her and the others to "catch up."

Pammy returned from the climb with a profound love for the woman who was going to be Sammy's wife—not someone who was too girlish, but a wonderful young woman who was ready to be a wife.

Now, in the West Train Station, Pammy felt good knowing that a way had been found for Karl to accompany her to the wedding in America. But how had he done it? It seemed impossible. There was the cost … and a passport for him. How had he done it? It was like a miracle.

Pammy knew Karl well enough to be certain that whatever he had worked out, she wasn't going to learn the details in the short time left before her train would be leaving. She told herself that it was just like Karl to wait until a few minutes before the departure of her train to spring this marvelous surprise. She would be a bundle of excitement until she got back from Paris. She knew Karl must have planned it that way. Yes, most definitely, that was just like him.

Giddy in her happiness, Pammy stared intently around. Many times she had been in the West Train Station. For the past year, at least once every month or two, she'd had to go to Paris or some other city. She focused her attention on Karl. Right now, right at this moment, while pretending to be oblivious to what was going on around him, he was monitoring things in the train station. She wanted to say, *Pay attention to me!* She wanted to demand that Karl tell her in a quick, simple way how he had arranged the trip to America.

But something was happening.

Pammy knew it in an instant. Karl's face that could conceal so much stopped concealing anything. He came erect and stared far back toward the rear of the train station; his entire body became tense.

At first, Pammy couldn't tell what it was that had captured Karl's attention. All she could see was the bustling crowd. Countless people wandering around the train station. But continuing to follow Karl's line of sight, she saw that he was focused on two men greeting each other. She couldn't tell which of the two men had been the one to arrive and which was doing the welcoming. After a moment, an American soldier with a camera came over and took a picture of the two men. These days the Americans and Russians were taking pictures of all the people arriving in Vienna by train. The British were more selective. They photographed only the ones who might be Jewish. The French made their presence known but seldom did any photographing.

Pammy stared hopelessly as Karl got to his feet and said, "Something important is going on here. I have to run."

"Important? What?"

"There are two people here who practice the profession of burglary."

"Burglars?"

"I have to run."

"Burglars? What about me?"

"I have to run. I have to follow those two men. See where they go."

And while Pammy watched helplessly, Karl went off on one of his police chases. For a moment, she was angry, but she couldn't hold onto the anger. It evaporated. For her, all that mattered was that in this crazy, mixed-up world, Karl was going to be with her at Sammy's wedding to the marvelous young woman named Jennifer.

BOOK TWO

Do Your Good or Lose It

Inside a Jail in Poland, October 1946

Sitting in a small room inside a Polish jail, pain-riddled Father Paskievich lowered his head. The badly beaten twenty-three-year-old priest was confused. He knew he needed to think, sort things out, but he became aware of a distracting noise, a dripping sound.

Drip ... drip ... drip.

Because he had lowered his head, blood from his injured nose was dropping onto the cement floor.

Drip ... drip ... drip.

He tried to ignore the dripping sound. He believed the important thing right now was for him to make sense of things. For a long time, his life had been good, but this morning when he left the priest house and began walking around in the church garden, he was suddenly jumped on by five characters who didn't identify themselves, didn't say anything, just did a lot of punching until they knocked him unconscious.

When he regained consciousness, he found himself in this small room in the jail. Now, standing near him were the five men who had jumped on him in the church garden. They were now wearing badges that identified them as Polish police. He wondered if he had been arrested because the Polish police had found out about the anti-Soviet things he was doing.

Why else would he have been jumped on, knocked unconscious, and taken to this jail?

He lifted his head. He realized someone was talking to him. He struggled to understand the words being spoken, but getting badly beaten had left him so confused.

Slowly, comprehension began taking hold. He knew the Polish police had been going around and finding people to sign a statement saying they were personally against everyone who was "an enemy of Mother Russia." The people who signed those statements were let go.

The statements were being collected and given to the Russians to show them that Polish people supported Soviet Russia. It was crazy, but these were crazy times.

He quickly signed the statement, but as soon as the policeman got his hands on the piece of paper, he laughed, and punching began again. Before lowering his head to avoid the full effect of the blows, Father Paskievich saw that two of the police seemed to be making a point of signifying to each other a low opinion of the policeman who got the statement and then started doing more punching. All five of the police had jumped on him in the church garden, but now he wondered if two of the five Polish police might be good men. Back in the church garden, when this trouble began, he would have declared that there was nothing but foulness in all five men beating on him, but at this moment he felt a positive feeling for two of the five policemen.

After being punched a few times, Father Paskievich came alert when one of the five policemen in the small room made what sounded like an announcement of some kind. His mind had cleared up quite a bit, and he realized he was being told to write out and sign a letter intended to get Police Inspector Karl Marbach to come from Vienna, Austria, to Poland where he could be arrested by Polish police. The letter was to state that the police inspector should go to a specifically identified Polish café for a meeting.

A draft of the letter Father Paskievich was expected to write and sign was handed to him. He knew if he wrote and signed the letter, it wouldn't draw Karl Marbach into a trap. There had been a meeting a few weeks ago during which he, Karl Marbach, the two Polder brothers, and a few others who had joined together against Soviet Russia had agreed that to keep safe, their future written communications would be sent to what they called secret addresses. Each of them would establish a secret address. Establishing secret addresses was just a matter of using addresses of trusted friends who would take care that letters with phony names on them would be kept safe until they could be passed on. When the messages were received by the ones they were intended for, they would always be read carefully, with knowledge that if the message wasn't highly important it wouldn't have been sent to the phony name at the secret address.

Father Paskievich wrote and signed the letter he knew would be mailed to Karl Marbach's regular address, and therefore would be recognized as not to be taken seriously.

Then he tried to focus his troubled mind. Late yesterday, he had learned that Marbach was planning to come to Poland. Apparently Marbach didn't know how quickly things had changed in the past few days, how dangerous it was for him to come to Poland. The thing to do was use a telephone to pass along a warning, but how do you do that when you are in jail?

Father Paskievich knew there was only one way to pass a warning to Marbach. The only way to pass a warning while in jail was to write out a letter addressed to Marbach's secret mailing address and somehow get the letter put in the mail. If Marbach read a letter sent to his secret address that contained a warning, he would cancel his plan to come to Poland from Vienna, Austria. If mailed promptly, such a letter would be delivered in time to keep Marbach safe. But how to get a letter mailed to Marbach at the secret mailing address in Vienna, Austria, while stuck here in a Polish jail? The only thing that might work was to try to get one of the two Polish police who seemed like they might be good men to put a letter in the mail. But would one of them agree to do that? Maybe. But only if it was an obscurely written letter, one that would not raise an alert from a Polish policeman who would obviously insist on reading a letter before possibly agreeing to mail it.

If Marbach got a letter containing an obscurely written warning, he would have no doubt it was valid if the letter was delivered to his secret address in Vienna, Austria, but what to put in what would have to be an obscurely written letter? A letter that would only be mailed if one of the two policemen agreed to mail it? Father Paskievich told himself the only thing for him to do was make it an innocuous—appearing letter, filled with friendly nonsense, addressed as though from one priest to another priest. But amidst a lot of nonsense, a letter could communicate what Marbach would recognize as a warning not to come to Poland. If Marbach knew there was danger, he would not come to Poland, and he would find a way to warn the Polder brothers and all the others who needed to be warned.

Father Paskievich knew he needed to think clearly if he was going to be able to write the kind of letter that needed to be written, filled with obscure nonsense, but containing what Marbach would recognize was a clear warning.

Think! Think!

Suddenly there was a noise from the hallway. Father Paskievich lifted his head and stared at the cell door. He watched the cell door open and Interrogator Rudnicki enter, accompanied by a guard. "We can't waste any more time," said Interrogator Rudnicki. "I have decided to make some recordings with your voice on them. On the telephone, the police inspector will think he is hearing you helplessly begging him to come to Poland so you can give him something highly important that can't be discussed over the telephone.

"It will be a very short telephone message. He will only hear a recording, but he will think it is a real telephone call, and he will waste no time coming to Poland. This is a trick that in various ways has worked before. We can make the recorder sound like you are personally on the phone, but it will only be a recording with words and statements we have teased out of you, words and statements that we will play over the telephone in any order we think is best based on what the police inspector is saying."

"I will not cooperate," said Father Paskievich. The way recorders worked these days, it seemed to him that it was best for him to refuse any cooperation. He was determined not to be a party to any activity intended to draw Marbach into a trap.

Interrogator Rudnicki didn't address Father Yakub Paskievich as a priest. Only the name was used. "Yakub Paskievich, I will have nothing less than your full cooperation."

Anticipating that the bad beating he had already received was going to get seriously worse, Father Paskievich began praying.

He prayed that he wouldn't yield to pain, that he wouldn't fail to do what he needed to do to keep Marbach safe.

Standing beside the guard, Interrogator Rudnicki said to Father Paskievich, "You will do as I want. I have a way to make you do what I want you to do. I have your sister. I have Wanda Paskievich. Her fate is in your hands."

Father Paskievich shook his head vigorously. "You have … my sister? That is impossible. My sister is dead in the war."

"Wanda Paskievich is alive."

"Wanda alive?" Father Paskievich shook his head. "Wanda alive?"

"Bring in the woman," Interrogator Rudnicki said to the guard.

Father Paskievich closed his eyes as the guard left the cell.

He opened his eyes a brief moment later when the guard returned with his hands on the shoulders of a very young woman the priest immediately recognized as his sister, the sister he hadn't seen for more than five years. The baby sister who for three years he had thought was dead.

"Wanda," he said, rising to his feet. He spoke his sister's name as though it was a prayer.

"Yakub," the young woman said while keeping her eyes focused on the floor. "They will put me in jail if you don't do this thing for them." She spoke with remoteness, like her words were rehearsed. Most likely they were.

"Wanda? You are alive." Father Yakub's voice was filled with wonder.

The young woman repeated her words. "They will put me in their awful jail if you don't do this thing for them." The same rehearsed sound in the voice, but as she lifted her face, her eyes filled with emotion. She stared, and her eyes spoke to Father Paskievich of the time in the recent past when they had been teenagers together, and he had been her trusted older brother.

"I thought you were dead," Father Paskievich said, staring at his sister's face, the face of a mature, young woman, but a face as precious to him as her childhood face had been.

Animation captured the youthful face. Wanda lifted and dropped her arms. Her voice no longer contained a rehearsed sound. "Yakub, remember, oh, please remember the pledge you used to make all those years ago.

"That pledge is precious to me at this moment. *Do your good or lose it.* They were words you used to speak when we were close together. At this moment, I am asking you to be as I remember you were when we were teenagers together. If you have something good you feel you need to do, I want you to do it."

"Do my good ...?" Father Paskievich's mind registered how courageous his sister was, given that she was facing jail, to remind him of the pledge he used to make to her when they were teenagers. *Do your good or lose it* was a pledge he had found on a piece of paper that had been left for anyone to pick up in a Vienna coffeehouse, left to be picked up like countless pieces of paper that were left to be picked up by strangers in coffeehouses.

Interrogator Rudnicki made a loud statement. "Prisoner Wanda Paskievich, you will be sent to jail unless your brother agrees to help us."

The young woman stared at her brother. "Yakub ..."

"Wanda, they want me to do something bad."

Wanda spoke in a firm voice. "If it is something bad they want you to do, of course you won't do it. You are my brother. You must hold onto your good. To hold onto your good, you must do the good in you."

Father Paskievich marveled at the wonderful young woman who was his sister. "Do my good," he affirmed to her. "Do my good or lose it."

"This is out of my hands," said Interrogator Rudnicki.

"*Do your good or lose it,*" Wanda said to her brother.

"God bless you, Wanda," Father Paskievich said to his sister.

An angry look captured the face of Interrogator Rudnicki. He said, "I am out of patience." Without saying anything more, he seized Wanda roughly by her arm and pushed her out the door.

The cell door slammed with a loud sound.

Father Paskievich sat down limply. After a few moments, one of the two police who was possibly a good man entered.

In despair, Father Paskievich looked at the Polish policeman he hoped was going to turn out to be a decent man. Wondering if he was engaging in something hopeless, he picked up a piece of paper and wrote an obscurely written letter addressed to an imaginary priest. When finished, he scribbled Marbach's secret mailing address on the piece of paper and made a beckoning motion to the Polish policeman.

The Polish policeman said, "If you want me to mail a letter for you, I will have to look at it first."

Father Paskievich showed the Polish policeman the letter and prayed long and hard.

The Polish policeman glanced at the letter and said, "Ah, a letter to another priest. Let me see … well, it looks all right. I can put this letter in the mail for you."

BOOK THREE

Four Guest-Friends

Early on an April day in 1938, one week after approval of the Anschluss, the incorporation of Austria into the Greater Reich, Vienna Police Inspector Karl Marbach was wondering how bad things were going to get now that the Nazis had total power. Alone in his lover's flat, Karl was standing in front of a bookcase that contained a gramophone collection. He stepped forward, fussed around, found the album he was looking for, withdrew one record platter, placed it on the gramophone, and then laid out on a table the dozen or more additional platters in the album. It took a lot of platters to play all of Beethoven's *Pastoral*.

While listening to the symphony, he went to a chair and sat down. From time to time, he had to get up to replace a platter. He hadn't arranged the platters, so the music wasn't played in the correct order. But he didn't care. Regardless of what order the platters were played in, all of it was the *Pastoral*. He had just fixed a platter to play when he heard familiar sounds in the hallway. He went quickly to the door and pulled it open.

Directly in front of him was his lover, Constanze Tandler. This was her flat, at least for the time being. She was Italian, an established actress in Italy who often performed in France and was currently playing the lead in a production at Vienna's Volkstheater. Constanze was fluent in several languages.

Eighteen-year-old Marianne Frish, a stranger to the flat, was holding Constanze's hand. Standing behind them was Anna Krassny, who was born and raised in Vienna. Like Constanze, Anna was an actress. Anna usually performed at Vienna's Burgtheater. In recent weeks, Constanze and Anna had become close friends.

Marianne's large, brown eyes brightened as she listened to the music playing on the gramophone. Her head began weaving in delighted response to what she recognized as a carefree tune in Beethoven's *Pastoral*. Karl grasped the teenager's hand, pressed it to his mouth, and drew her forward. She smiled shyly. Karl smiled back in a reassuring manner and then shifted his attention to Constanze and Anna. While he watched, Anna stared at him, took one step backward as though to gain momentum, then rushed forward.

No hand kiss would suffice for Anna. She demanded a hug and got it. Then she demanded a kiss on the mouth and got it. A few years ago, they had been lovers. Now there were no romantic feelings between them, but their friendship was strong.

Anna drew her head back to peer over her shoulder at Constanze. Anna was Karl's former lover, and Constanze was his current lover. The two women exchanged smiles.

While Anna returned her attention to Karl, Constanze remained standing in the doorway with a broad-brimmed hat pushed back on her head.

Anna laughed a throaty laugh, pulled Karl close, and said over her shoulder, "Constanze, if you had not become such a good friend to me in recent weeks, I would take this man away from you."

Constanze acknowledged the joke by sticking out her tongue at Anna. Then she turned toward Marianne and said, "Sweet one, dear sweet one, please find some drinks to freshen us. There is some marvelous Schilcher Rose for those of us who have the taste to appreciate good wine. I assume that includes you. As for this oafish man, give him a glass of his schnapps—his kümmel."

Anna joined Marianne at a cabinet near the far side of the room to prepare the drinks. They found four glasses and set them on the top of the cabinet: three long-stemmed, crystal-clear wine glasses for the women, and a plain, flat-bottomed glass for the man. While the drinks were being prepared, Karl stared at Constanze, who was still standing in the doorway. Her head and shoulders were moving in time to the gaiety in Beethoven's music spilling forth from the gramophone.

Karl walked across the room, took Constanze by the arm, and led her over to the sofa. They were still settling themselves on the sofa when Marianne walked up to them holding a tray upon which were drinks. Karl reached out and secured for Constanze a long-stemmed wine glass filled with Schilcher Rose. He handed it to her and then took from the tray the plain, flat-bottomed glass containing his kümmel.

Anna walked over, retrieved from the tray a glass filled with Schilcher Rose, and made herself comfortable in a heavily stuffed chair facing the sofa.

After setting aside the tray, Marianne took a glass of Schilcher Rose for herself and sat at the far end of the sofa.

Drawing Karl's arm close around her, Constanze lifted her glass and proclaimed an ancient Greek toast, a very special celebration of hospitality she reserved only for people to whom she felt a close bond: "Guest-Friends!"

Anna held up her glass and echoed the toast: "Guest-Friends!"

Marianne looked puzzled, but lifted her glass and spoke the toast: "Guest—Friends!"

With one arm around Constanze, Karl used his free hand to raise his glass. He spoke the toast with solemn deliberation: "Guest-Friends!"

With the ancient Greek toast completed, Anna decided to indulge playful mischief. "Well, Marianne, because you and I haven't seen much of each other before, and because we are now Guest-Friends, I will share with you a secret. The secret I shall share with you is about Karl. I want you to know that Karl is successful with women because he is willing to be a little afraid of them."

"I make no secret of it," Karl said. "Without some fear, there is no awe, and without awe, it is impossible for a man to fully appreciate a woman."

Constanze and Anna shared a glance and began laughing. Anna's deep, throaty laughter joined with Constanze's distinctive E-flat laughter, and a melody was created. Marianne's playful giggling leavened the melody.

Karl shook his head and drew his arm more tightly around Constanze. He nodded appreciatively when she maneuvered around until she was able to rest her head on his chest. Her E-flat laughter continued.

Standing alone, Marianne stopped giggling long enough to say to Constanze, "I haven't told you yet, but I got a letter today from my boyfriend, Emile, who is off visiting some business friends in France. I have told you that Emile and I met at the Musikverein. That was six months ago. You have never told me … I wonder … where did you and the police inspector …?"

Constanze placed her hand on her lover's stomach and said to Marianne, "We are Guest-Friends. Don't call him police inspector. You may call him Karl or Guest-Friend, but nothing else. Not tonight. Not in this place. Guest-Friendship requires equality. Now, to answer the question you were starting to ask, Karl and I met in the Café Central last year."

Karl looked down at Constanze's hand. He hoped she was going to keep it on his stomach. He said to Marianne, "The first time I saw Constanze was not one year ago. It was ten years earlier. She was on the stage right here in Vienna, playing the part of Margarethe in *Faust*. I must say I never saw any other actress play the part of that handmaid of goodness with such expressive femininity."

Constanze lifted her head. She kept her hand on Karl's stomach as she said to Marianne, "In the play, Margarethe is virtuous but not timid. It is a common mistake to portray Margarethe as the timid handmaid of goodness."

"The night I saw it," Karl said, "you made her sensuality very obvious." He knew that. Constanze was proud of having played the part that way.

"Oh, what a great play!" Marianne exclaimed to Constanze. "I wish I had seen you in it. *Faust* is one of my very favorite plays."

Karl looked at Constanze and playfully spoke one of the immortal lines from *Faust*. "The eternal feminine image that leads men on." He made a pretended gasp when Constanze shoved her elbow against his ribs.

Leaning back in the chair facing the sofa, Anna laughed cheerily.

Constanze said, "Soon the play I am doing will close, and it doesn't look like I will be doing another play in Vienna any time soon. In order to continue to do theater work in Vienna, I would be required to sign one of those terrible pieces of paper saying I am not a Jew."

With wide-open eyes, Marianne asked Constanze, "Why don't you sign the awful piece of paper? I am Jewish, but you don't have any Jewish blood in you."

"Come, now, Marianne," Anna said, "would you have Constanze do anything that gives support to the evil notion that there is something wrong with having Jewish blood?"

Marianne stirred herself to an upright position at the end of the sofa. "I am a Jew." Immediately, she looked unsure of herself.

Constanze didn't miss a beat. "I am a Red."

Anna was quick to chime in. "I am a Habsburger."

Karl laughed as he said, "I am a police inspector."

They all laughed. There was nothing else to do but laugh. They laughed joyful laughter that bound together four Guest-Friends.

BOOK FOUR

Walking Down the Street

A man and a woman were walking down a street early in the evening. It might have been many years ago, or it might be today. The city might be Columbus, Ohio, or Paris, France, or Vienna, Austria.

The man grasped the woman's wrist—not her hand, but her wrist—and carefully began moving her arm in a swinging motion.

The woman smiled. The man was her husband. She liked what he was doing with her arm. He often chose to walk this way with her. In a coquettish voice, she said, "I am letting you hold my wrist and swing my arm, but don't get any ideas."

"You have a marvelous wrist. I am fascinated by your wrist."

"I have never known a man like you."

"You are more like all the women I have ever known than any other woman I have ever known."

"Oh … behave yourself. If you behave yourself, when we get home, I may make supper for you."

"I'm sorry. I'll take you home, but I'll have to leave right away. There is police work I have to do."

The woman bristled angrily. "How late will you be coming home tonight?"

"I may be very late."

The woman said, "I never should have married a man who does police work."

"I am blessed to be able—for however long it lasts—to hold the wrist of a woman like you."

The woman made an anguished sound, grabbed the hand holding her wrist, stopped walking, pulled herself into the man's arms, and kissed him.

They continued kissing while people walked past them.

Finally, the man drew the woman's head back, kissed her face one more time, then drew her hand upward, stared at it like he was marveling at a treasure, and pressed the hand against his mouth.

A few moments later, the woman withdrew her wrist from the man's hand and inquired, "Will you try to get home at a reasonable hour?"

"I'll try, but I may be late. I may be very late. Don't wait up."

Without speaking any more words, they resumed walking. Again, the man grasped the woman's wrist with his hand and gently swung her arm.

BOOK FIVE

Getting Ready for Work in Vienna in 1945

On Monday, August 6, 1945, the war in Europe was over, and in occupied Vienna, Austria, Captain Theodore Millican was almost ready to begin his workday. Millican was assigned to the American housekeeping force in Vienna, Austria, because he could speak German, which was close enough to Viennese for a high-level decision maker in the US military to decide to send him to Vienna. He had learned the German from his Munich-born mom. He always called her "Mom." His Irish-American father, whom he always addressed as "Pa," had been, in Pa's own words, "bumming around" in Europe at the end of World War I when Pa met Mom. In November of 1918, a few days after Pa and Mom met, they got married in a Munich church. Church protocol was not rigorously enforced in those chaotic days.

A few weeks after the marriage, Pa brought his German bride, along with the bride's mother, to Cleveland, Ohio, and presented them to the Cleveland Millicans, a tightknit Irish tribe. For the Cleveland Millicans, one of their own returning after the war with a German girl and the German girl's mother was difficult to accept at first. But full acceptance did come; the girl and her mother were, after all, Catholic. For the Millicans, it was best to be Irish and Catholic, but as images of the First World War faded, the Cleveland Millicans deemed people to be all right if they were German and Catholic.

Millican always thought of himself as Irish, even though his mom, when he was a kid, taught him German right along with English and was always taking him to one of the many German activities in Cleveland. As a boy, he accepted things as they came. His pals in the Catholic schools were mostly

Irish, but he also had friends who were French, Italian, and other Catholic ethnicities. Pals outside of school included Jews. Ira Bernstein was a close pal. But he had no Protestant close pals until he joined the Cleveland Police Force. At first—on the force—Protestants were hard ones for him to figure, but it didn't take him long to learn that most of the Protestants were all right. Some of them became close pals. And he got lucky on the force. It took him only seven years to make detective. It helped that he played a key part in a shootout that got his picture in the newspapers.

From the time Millican was a kid, he had known he was blessed. He loved his pa—the mounted Cleveland policeman, the large policeman on a horse, the loud, bellowing Irishman who was tough, maybe sometimes too tough, but always fair, always a man to look up to and respect. And Millican loved his German mom totally and completely. As for his treasured German grandma, it was impossible not to love the wonderful, old woman who in recent years struggled against growing confusion. A lot of confusion. In the year before Millican began army service, Grandma knew who her daughter was and remembered some things from her life as a young girl in Germany, but not much more.

Shortly before beginning his military service, Millican often sat with Grandma. He drank glasses of tea with her, listened, talked, and kept her company. She spoke to him in German, occasionally startling him by unexpectedly breaking into song. When that happened, she sang in a clear, pure voice. The German songs were beautiful, most of them filled with tales of love and romance and foolishness. Afterward, she would talk about wonderful boys of her youth. It was amazing to hear stories of youthful love from someone who had always seemed beyond that sort of thing. And there was something else Grandma sometimes talked about: those she called Yids. She no longer called them Jews, like she had before the confusion started. In her confusion, the stories she told about Jews were strong and filled with scorn. It was painful for Millican to listen to Grandma talk in a way he had never heard her speak before the confusion.

At his final farewell party before going into military service, there was Sally, the wonderful woman who had become his wife. In addition, there was kid brother, Eddie, and younger sister, Beth, who came up from Columbus, skipping classes at Ohio State University to be at the farewell. Also very much present were Pa and Mom and Grandma. And uncles, aunts, cousins, some neighborhood people, and, of course, cop pals.

When the farewell party was nearly done, he stared shyly at the group gathered around in the living room of his parents' house before yielding to calls for him to kiss Sally. She was a treasure, a wonderful Irish-American girl. After kissing Sally, he turned to his mom, grasped her tightly, and whispered German words in her ear.

And then there was Grandma, the old woman, deep in her confusion, so much of her memory gone. She clasped him in tight desperation and exclaimed in German: "Oh, Theodore. You are Theodore. I love you so much, Theodore."

He replied in German, "I love you, Grandma."

Finally, after separating from Grandma, he solemnly shook Pa's hand. It was then, in the living room of the house, that Pa drew him away from the others for a few moments and said with more solemnity than emotion, "Be good." Those words were expected. Pa was always saying "Be good" to him and his brother and his sister. But at the farewell party, after saying, "Be good," Pa said in a quiet voice that only he could hear, "You're going off to war, Ted. I know you'll do your duty. But there's something you ought to be told. A couple of times in the past few days, I wanted to tell you something and kept putting it off, but now time is running out. What I want to say to you, Ted, is find your good and hold onto it with your fingers as tight as you can. You'll never have a firmer hold on your good than by your fingers. If you lose your grip on your good in the days that are coming, grab for it. And keep grabbing for it. That's the difference between a good man and a guy who's just getting by. A good man holds onto his good with his fingers, or he's out there grabbing."

At the time, Millican thought that was an odd thing for Pa to say.

A few hours later, at the train station, the folks left him and Sally alone on the platform, and he and Sally faced each other. She hugged him fiercely, almost lost control. He told her he loved her. That was all he said. He didn't tell her he felt lost in the fragrance surrounding her.

Afterward—during the war—Sally's letters to him had that same fragrance on them. But for the last year, her letters had a different fragrance, not the fragrance he remembered from 1942, three and a half years ago.

Again and again, he had asked himself a simple question: what kind of world keeps a man away from his wife for three and a half years?

This was August of 1945. He hadn't seen Sally since their farewell early in 1942. Sally gave birth to their kid a few weeks after he shipped off to North Africa in the late fall of 1942. He had never seen little George, except in baby pictures sent by Sally.

After North Africa, there had been battlefields from Anzio all the way to the Rhine. One of the things that helped him deal with the things that happened on battlefields was what Pa had told him at the farewell about holding onto his good by his fingers instead of being out there grabbing for it. There were moments when all he heard in his head was "Keep grabbing for it."

Kid brother, Eddie, had followed him into the service. Eddie enlisted in late 1943, immediately after his eighteenth birthday.

Millican spent most of 1943 in Italy. He got his battlefield promotion in Italy, accepting the silver bars even though that meant leaving Company B. As an infantry officer, first as a lieutenant and then as a captain, he learned that you never do enough. An especially painful thing was writing letters with awkwardly chosen words to convey to wives and sweethearts and mothers and fathers something personal about men who had been killed or badly wounded. Oddly, it was always harder writing letters to families of soldiers he didn't really know than to the loved ones of close buddies. Why was that? Could anybody explain that?

When the war was nearly over, there was the liberation of the concentration camps. Those god-awful Nazi concentration camps.

But finally the war was over. The war was over, and he had a bunch of medals: Purple Heart, Bronze Star, the Distinguished Service Cross. And the medal that counted the most to him, maybe the only medal that counted at all: the Combat Infantryman's Badge, the CBI.

Eddie had made it through the war, too. And the kid had his own CBI. What a guy, that kid!

But no more time to think about that now. Right now, the thing to do was totally concentrate on the business at hand. This was a Monday, and for sure there would be housekeeping work to do this day.

BOOK SIX

On the Way to a 1945 Meeting

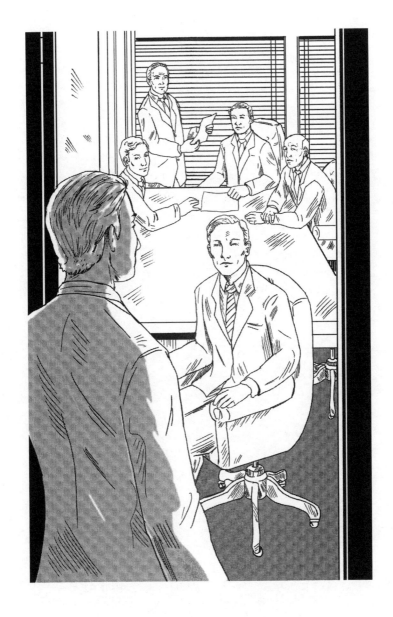

Vienna, Austria—Saturday, August 4, 1945

Former SS Major Stephan Kaas walked quickly along the Vienna Ringstrasse. He was on his way to a meeting with the Amis. As usual, he used the colloquialism "Amis" to identify Americans. Yesterday, on the telephone, he had initiated a brief telephone conversation with Amis, and they had invited him to meet with them in person.

Now, moving quickly, Kaas looked around on the Ringstrasse, the great boulevard circling the inner city of Vienna. An offensive stench was rising from smashed buildings and abandoned litter. He had known that same stench fighting against enemies of the Reich in Russia, in Hungary, in Poland, and finally in Czechoslovakia.

While moving at the fast pace, something captured his attention: a temporary wooden structure. The wooden structure was a shed used by street workers. As he came alongside the shed, he saw painted in large English letters: Kilroy Was Here.

He scowled. He knew enough English to figure out what the words said, but why were the Amis printing those words with chalk or paint on every available wall, post, or window? The idiocy showed that the Amis were strange creatures—strange creatures, indeed.

As Kaas edged forward, something important caught his attention. Near the end of the shed were wanted posters. Hand-painted Soviet wanted posters, each individually painted by an Ivan or by one of the hired persons working for the Ivans.

Quickly, he established that his name and picture weren't on any of the wanted posters. There was no wanted poster for former SS Major Stephan Kaas, but one of the hand-painted pictures on a poster caught his attention. He read what was printed under the picture.

The Soviets will provide 5,000 premium cigarettes in exchange for the traitor and renegade who is former Vienna Police Inspector Karl Marbach.

Kaas studied the wanted poster for Karl Marbach. They looked a lot alike and had very similar facial features. The facial similarity was clear because the wanted poster had a hand-painted picture of Karl Marbach. Black and white photographs on wanted posters could be terribly ambiguous, whereas hand-painted pictures could be eerily lifelike.

Kaas reviewed his history with Karl Marbach. For a while they had been close friends, but at the last sight of each other in 1938 they had become enemies. Now, Karl Marbach had a reward of 5,000 cigarettes on his head. Kaas smiled. Karl Marbach must have done something significant to get the Ivans agitated enough to offer 5,000 cigarettes. That was a lot of cigarettes, even if it was substantially less than the 20,000 cigarettes offered as a reward for the capture of former SS Major Stephan Kaas.

These days, cigarettes were more dependable for buying things than currency, even Ami currency. For 5,000 cigarettes, a person could live comfortably for a year. Five thousand cigarettes was enough to pay for a place to live for year and also provide food and other amenities.

While continuing his walk along the Ringstrasse, Kaas recalled how tight his friendship with Karl Marbach had been before it turned sour. In March of 1938, after the Anschluss, the annexation of Austria into the Greater Reich, he had come down from Berlin to take the job as chief of Vienna Kripo—Vienna Criminal Police—and among the many men subordinate to him was Police Inspector Karl Marbach. Very quickly, working closely together, they became like comrade soldiers. The comrade soldier bond was a vital bond. Kaas had first experienced it in the trenches during 1914, 1915, 1916, 1917, and 1918. After the war, doing police work in Berlin in the 1920s and 1930s, he had enjoyed several strong friendships, but never anything close to the comrade soldier bond. And then the comrade soldier bond came quickly when he and Karl Marbach worked together in 1936, beginning with a case that entailed a certain amount of risk. But the comrade soldier bond with Karl Marbach didn't last. It was unusual for the comrade soldier bond to ever be lost, but it came apart when Karl Marbach's lover, Volkstheater actress Constanze Tandler, was killed by National Socialists on a drunken rampage. The killing was awful, but Karl Marbach caused trouble for a prominent National Socialist family linked with the killing, and it became a matter of duty to bring to a halt the harm Karl Marbach was causing. Kaas believed that one must always put duty above personal relationships, even a personal relationship as strong as the comrade soldier bond.

As things turned out, Karl Marbach was put under arrest but escaped.

Kaas shook his head. Thinking about Constanze Tandler brought forth the painful memory of Anna Krassny, the love of his life, the strongest love he had ever known. Both Constanze and Anna had been Volkstheater actresses. Now both of them were dead.

Kaas plunged his hands into his suit coat pockets. Nineteen thirty-eight was a long time ago. Seven years? Yes, seven years. But it might as well have been seven centuries. Countless lifetimes separated 1938 from 1945.

Kaas shook his mind free of intruding thoughts and focused his attention on the meeting he was going to have with the Amis. If everything worked out as he hoped, the Amis would take him off their wanted list, and off the British and French wanted lists as well. After that was done, he would be on his way to a good, new life in the strange postwar world of 1945.

He thought about the good, new life he was determined to find, but he also affirmed that he would never reject the beautiful dream called National Socialism. He believed Adolf Hitler had started off good, especially with the way Jews were dealt with, but terrible mistakes had been made fighting the war. Still, he told himself, he had no regrets for having fully and faithfully served National Socialism.

Lowering his head, Kaas resolved to stop thinking about the past. He concentrated his thoughts on the future, the good, new life he believed was awaiting him, and continued his fast, forward march on the Ringstrasse.

But suddenly he came to a halt. In his path, a few paces in front of him, were two Ivan soldiers. For him, Ivans were "un-animals"—creatures lower than animals, creatures that didn't deserve the consideration that might be given to a dog.

He sized up the situation. The two Ivans, both of them wearing big balloon trousers, looked drunk and dangerous, but they didn't appear to be carrying any weapons. It wasn't unusual to see Ivans without weapons. It was routine for Ivans on leave status in Vienna not to carry a weapon.

Kaas stepped aside, but that didn't help. The two Ivans made it clear he had their attention. They gave out a shout in Russian.

They shouted more Russian words.

Kaas was pretty sure what they wanted. They wanted him to give up his wristwatch, which was visible on his left wrist. The two Ivans were demanding that his wristwatch be surrendered.

One of the two Ivans, a creature of ordinary size, moved forward and stood directly in front of him. It was a question of yielding his wristwatch or engaging the two Ivans in a fight. Kaas made his decision and immediately concentrated on how he would handle the fight. The important thing was to get off the first punch, hopefully the first few punches.

Kaas moved his mind ahead of the flow of the action, as he always did when he was in a fight or any sort of physical struggle. He took measure of the space around him and the position of each of the two Ivans within that space. Then he made a quick movement that momentarily placed him one step to the left side of the Ivan standing directly in front of him. In that instant, he calculated direction and the speed of movement for him and for each of the Ivans, then quickly moved forward and delivered a blow at the first Ivan, the one standing in front of him. It was a fast blow but hard enough to get the job done. It knocked the first Ivan off balance and set the creature up for a finishing blow that was forcefully delivered.

The first Ivan fell helplessly onto the sidewalk.

Now, it was a matter of the second Ivan.

Kaas sized up the second Ivan, a powerful-looking creature with hatred on his Slavic face. A jabbing left fist was used to push the un-animal off balance, and the hatred was replaced by fear. Kaas felt good seeing the fear. A follow-up punch produced a distinct cracking sound from the exposed jaw. A third blow drove the Ivan down onto the cement, where he made a rolling motion before collapsing into unconsciousness.

Five deft blows dealt to two Ivans, and it was all over.

Kaas savored a good feeling. He had seen the hatred in enemy eyes become fear, and he had smashed two Ivans into helplessness.

Quickly, people began gathering around. The small group included a woman with a child, two young men, an old lady, and a man and a woman who looked like they might be married. Kaas glanced at the onlookers.

For Kaas, this moment was good. He liked seeing the looks on the faces of these Viennese civilians, hearing their voices express approval for what had been done to the Ivans. There was only one sour note: those who can stare at you and speak words of praise can also betray.

Kaas quickly moved on, but the voices expressing praise lingered in his ears as he continued on his way to the meeting with the Amis.

42665778R00068

Made in the USA
Lexington, KY
04 July 2015